Long Fin Silver

READ ALL THE SHARK SCHOOL BOOKS!

#1: Deep-Sea Disaster

#2: Lights! Camera! Hammerhead!

#3: Squid-napped!

#4: The Boy Who Cried Shark

#5: A Fin-tastic Finish

#6: Splash Dance

#7: Tooth or Dare

#8: Fishin': Impossible

SHARK SCHOOL

#9 Long Fin Silver

BY DAVY OCEAN
ILLUSTRATED BY AARON BLECHA

ALADDIN   New York   London   Toronto   Sydney   New Delhi

WITH THANKS TO PAUL EBBS

ALADDIN

An imprint of Simon & Schuster Children's Publishing Division
1230 Avenue of the Americas, New York, NY 10020
First Aladdin hardcover edition February 2018
Text copyright © 2018 by Hothouse Fiction
Illustrations copyright © 2018 by Aaron Blecha
Also available in an Aladdin paperback edition.
All rights reserved, including the right of reproduction in whole or in part in any form.
ALADDIN and related logo are registered trademarks of Simon & Schuster, Inc.
For information about special discounts for bulk purchases, please contact
Simon & Schuster Special Sales at 1-866-506-1949 or business@simonandschuster.com.
The Simon & Schuster Speakers Bureau can bring authors to your live event. For more
information or to book an event contact the Simon & Schuster Speakers Bureau at 1-866-248-3049
or visit our website at www.simonspeakers.com.
Series designed by Karin Paprocki
Interior designed by Mike Rosamilia
The text of this book was set in Write Demibd.
Manufactured in the United States of America 0118 FFG
2 4 6 8 10 9 7 5 3 1
Library of Congress Control Number 2017958772
ISBN 978-1-4814-6553-3 (hc)
ISBN 978-1-4814-6552-6 (pbk)
ISBN 978-1-4814-6554-0 (eBook)

Long Fin Silver

CHAPTER 1

"Avast ye, me hearties!!!!!!!!!!!!" I yell as I pounce into my seabedroom and begin searching for my suitcase.

"A vast what?" Humphrey my humming-fish alarm clock says, peering at Larry my lantern fish's rear dorsal. "I wouldn't say it was vast. Large,

maybe. You should cut down on the Kelp Krispies, Larry."

"Hey!" says Larry, angrily flashing his light. "You're not so slim yourself!"

"Shiver me timbers!" I whoop as I tail-swipe a suitcase from under my bed. I bump it open with the right side of my hammerhead and dart over to my drawers. "Don't you two know what day it is?"

"The day you go bonkers?" says Humphrey.

"No!" I swim up to them and put one fin over my eye like a patch and wave my tail in their faces like a sword. "It's

the day I'm off to Treasure Reef for our
family vacation!"

I start pulling clothes from my drawers. "Treasure Reef is the best vacation
destination in the whole sea world! It's

like the pirate paradise of the ocean and we're going there for two weeks! I wish you two could join us, but Dad and Mom said just Ralph could come this time."

Humphrey and Larry just look bored.

Ding!!!!

That's me having an idea.

I now know *exactly* how to make the trip to Treasure Reef seem more interesting to them—I'll make a list!

"Number one: LONG FIN SILVER!" I blurt at Humphrey and Larry.

"Who?" they both say.

"Number one: Long Fin Silver was the greatest pirate of the seas!"

LONG FIN SILVER

"Greatest parrot?" says Larry.

"No! Pirate!"

"Oh, I thought you meant one of those funny-faced parrot fish," says Larry.

"NO! Number one: Long Fin Silver was

the meanest villain of the low seas! He rode his poop-decked submarine, the *Barracuda*. . . . Why are you laughing?"

"Keep going!" says Humphrey, holding his fin to his side as he giggles.

Poop Deck

THE BARRACUDA

"Why have you stopped?" Larry giggles.

"You're both laughing because I said 'poop' aren't you?"

The two fish nod and roll onto their backs. Bubbles of laughter stream from their mouths.

"A poop deck is a special deck at the back of a pirate submarine where the captain stands and commands his pirates as they attack ships to steal their treasure!"

"Are you sure it's not where they put the toilet?" Humphrey is barrel rolling now, bumping into Larry and sending him spinning across the room.

"So, I suppose you don't want me to tell you about the legend of the lost treasure, then?"

Humphrey and Larry stop mid-giggle.

"Treasure?" they both say, floating the right way up.

"Number one: Before he died, Long Fin Silver is said to have—"

"Why do you keep saying number one?" Larry interrupts.

"Because I'm trying to give you a list!" I sigh. "Number one: Before he died, Long Fin Silver is said to have buried the Black Blood Pearl somewhere on Treasure Reef. . . ."

"The Black Blood Pearl?" Humphrey's eyes are as wide as starfish pies. "What's that?"

"The most valuable and beautiful pearl in the history of the ocean. Stolen from the very neck of the baroness of sharks on the day of her wedding to the king of sand!"

"Wow!" say Humphrey and Larry in unison.

"Number two: Silver led a daring raid beneath Hook Bay to steal the pearl before the baroness could say 'I do.'"

"What did she say instead?" Larry asks.

"'I don't—obviously. But that's not all. Number three: The king of sand chased Long Fin Silver to the ends of the ocean, twice round and back again, because the

baroness wouldn't marry him until he returned the Black Blood Pearl to her neck!"

"And did he?" Humphrey asks.

"No!"

"Number four: Long Fin Silver, the smartest pirate who has ever swam the seas, was never, ever caught by the king of sand!"

"But what did he do with the Black Blood Pearl?" Larry asks.

"Number five: Legend says he buried it on Treasure Reef! But although the king of sand searched the reef for the rest of his life, he never, ever found the pearl and so he never, ever married the baroness of sharks."

"You have got to be kidding!" Humphrey yells.

"Number six: No. And that's where I'm going on vacation! So I have decided that I, Harry Hammerskull, of Shark Point, will be the one who finally finds the Black Blood Pearl. And I'll go down

in history as the greatest and smartest treasure hunter of all time."

"How will you find it when no one else has?" Larry asks.

I wait for the *ding* of a new idea. . . . But it doesn't come.

"I haven't quite worked that part out yet."

Before they can start laughing again, I

quickly finish packing and close my suit-case with a firm, fast *click!*

"Who on earth is Harry Hammerskull?"

I almost jump out of my sharkskin as I spin around.

Phew!

It's only Ralph.

He must have swum in through my window while I was telling my list to Humphrey and Larry.

Ralph bumps into my face, climbs into my mouth, and starts moving about pick-ing bits of breakfast out from between my teeth.

Ralph is my pilot fish toothbrush. He's

also my best friend in the whole ocean. I have to tell you that a toothbrush who is also your best friend is totally *COOL-WEIRDCOOLWEIRDCOOL!*

Ralph is chipping starfish crunch off my teeth and gobbling it down. "I said, who is Harry Hammerskull?"

"MMMMPHMMMMPPMMMMMMMMMPHHH!" I reply.

"What?" says Ralph, sticking his nose back out.

I spit him out, happy that my teeth feel lovely and clean. "I said it's my pirate name. Harry Hammerskullandcrossbones. Hammerskull for short."

"You really are letting this Treasure Reef vacation go to your head, aren't you?"

I stare at Ralph. "This is going to be the best vacation we've ever had, me hearty. Arrrgh!!"

Ralph puts his face in his fins, not too impressed with my pirate talk.

"Harry-Warry-Wooo-Wah! It's time to go!"

I cringe as Mom calls upstairs to me. She'd better not call me that while we're away. It's the least pirate name ever.

Ralph and I swim downstairs. The hallway is stuffed with suitcases and bags and backpacks of all sizes.

Mom is floating by the door, checking her watch and making sure her summer hat is on straight.

I hold up my suitcase and drift past her, where I see a taxicrab waiting to take us to Shark Point Harbor.

"Did you remember to pack those books for Cousin Harvey?" Mom asks.

I nod and hold up a net-bag full of books.

Harvey and my aunt Hettie and uncle Hector are also coming on vacation. I haven't seen Harvey since he was a baby. I remember him looking at me all googly-eyed and hugging me and gurgling my name. He thinks I'm the greatest. It'll be loads of fun seeing him again and getting him to join me and Ralph.

I quickly make a list of my fellow pirates in my head and give them pirate names:

1. Wrecker-Ralph
2. Harpoon-Humphrey *
   (Making sure all is safe on the home front)
   Landlubber-Larry *
   (Helping Harpoon-Humphrey make sure all is safe on the home front)

And my new sidekick

3.   High-Seas-Harvey!

I know Harvey is going to be the cool-est little cousin EVER!

CHAPTER 2

"Stop that, Harvey! Get away from the wheel!"

Aunt Hettie is pulling Harvey from the ferry's steering wheel and Uncle Hector is trying to stop Captain Pike, the ferry's commanding officer, from throwing us off his ship!

I float next to my dad, who is trying really hard not to be noticed. As the mayor of Shark Point, getting thrown off a ferry would not be good for his reputation.

"If this gets in the papers . . ." I hear him mutter.

Mom finally helps Hettie remove Harvey from the wheelhouse and we lead him downstairs to the deck. Uncle Hector apologizes to Captain Pike and says he will pay for "any damages."

When I'd been looking forward to seeing Harvey earlier, it hadn't occurred to me that baby sharks can sometimes grow up to be bratty, mischief-making, attention-seeking, pain-in-the-dorsal sharks!!!

The sweet little shark with the cute, googly eyes has turned into a massive bundle of trouble.

As soon as we boarded the whale-ferry he'd started yelling, "I wanna go there. I wanna go there!" pointing at the wheelhouse high on the whale's back.

Captain Pike, wanting to keep on the good side of Dad, had agreed immediately. As the whale-ferry started wafting his tail to gently move us away from the shore, Harvey had thrown himself at the wheel, turning it to the right and then left—sending the whale straight toward the side of another ferry! Mom and Auntie Hettie got him away just in time before we crashed.

Captain Pike and his crew regain control of the ferry, steering it down into the depths of Hook Bay. Harvey starts kicking and screaming, ordering his "mean mom" and "dorky dad" to take him home. All thoughts of him becoming an adoring member of my pirate crew float right out of my head.

Sigh.

"You're going to have to distract/
watch/take care of him," says Mom.

"Wait. What? Why?"

"You're the older cousin. It's up to you
to set a good example." Mom gives me
one of her stares. "This is everyone's
vacation, Harry, not just yours. I want you
to help give your aunt Hettie and uncle
Hector a break. Have you forgotten it's
their wedding anniversary? It's your job
to keep Harvey entertained for a while.
Do I make myself clear?"

I actually had forgotten it was my aunt
and uncle's anniversary. That was one of

the reasons why we were taking such a nice vacation in the first place. But I didn't like that watching Harvey was part of the deal.

"As a jellyfish," I say, huffing my way over to Harvey. I find Ralph wedged in his mouth, tail flapping furiously as Harvey tickles him under the fins.

Harvey's mouth is not yet big enough to have a pilot-fish toothbrush of his own—which is a surprise considering how much noise he can make.

I pull Ralph out of Harvey's mouth and hope for the *ding* of a new idea for what to do with the little brat.

Ralph shakes his head and straight-
ens out his fins. "I hate being tickled!"

Harvey just gives an evil grin and swims
toward Ralph. "I wanna toothbrush!"

I push Harvey back by his nose and
wave a stern fin at him. "Leave Ralph
alone, Harvey, or you'll be in big trouble."

"I'm not scared of you, Hammerskull.
You can't tell me what to do!"

But before I can answer, Ralph grabs
my fin and points to a poster on the wall.
"Look, Harry!"

Ding!

An idea pops into my head. The
colorful poster shows all the activities

on board the whale-ferry. In one corner there's an area full of waterslides, fin-ball hoops, and amusement arcades. It's called Fishfun Park!

This will definitely keep Harvey out of trouble.

And I'll be able to start my search for the Long Fin Silver Black.

Without High-Seas Harvey.

Fishfun Park does keep him busy.

For about eleven minutes.

Because that's how long it takes for Harvey to get himself banned from every ride in the place. He's driving me crazy!

I bet Long Fin Silver never had to put up with this from his crew. I bet if anyone stepped out of line he'd have them walk the plank. I don't know anyone who has ever walked any kind of plank, but I bet it's terrifying and I bet Harvey would behave himself if he had to do it.

Now that we're banned from all the rides and slides, the only place left to us is the amusement arcade. Leading the way over, I give Harvey some of the coins Mom gave us for krill-creams or floatdogs. "For the video games," I tell Harvey's disappearing backside. He moves so fast he creates a powerful backwash that spins Ralph like he's in a washing machine.

I grab Ralph's right fin but get caught up in his twisty tumble. I'm thrown through the water. I land fin up, right in front of a pod of girl dolphins.

They float to a stop. Giggling.

I get up, ready to tell them to stop . . .

When . . .

Well . . .

I . . .

OUCH!!!!!

Ralph twists to a stop and fins me in the side. "Harry! What's up?"

I . . .

31

"Harry! Your eyes. They've gone all wonky."

The rest of me has gone all wonky too. One of the dolphins is absolutely . . . totally . . . unbelievably . . .

"I've run out of words," I tell Ralph.

The pod moves past us, still giggling, and the dolphin who caused my epic word-fail looks back over her shoulder and smiles.

"Did you see that?" I shake Ralph by the shoulders. "She smiled at me. The one with the big eyes. She actually smiled. At *me*. My life is complete."

Ralph looks past me to the arcade. "Hmm, well, it's certainly a complete mess. Look!"

I look toward the arcade. A whale-ferry staff-squid is escorting Harvey out with one of his tentacles. "I'm sorry, young shark, but you have to leave. And not come back here. Ever."

Harvey fins his nose at the squid and dashes out of his tentacle reach—but he doesn't get very far. He smashes straight into the pod of girl dolphins, sending them spinning!

"Oh no!" I say, dashing over with Ralph.

I quickly grab two of the dolphins and Ralph hangs on to another for dear life.

As the girls slow down, I notice that I'm holding fins with the one who made me speechless before.

I float back in shock.

And then . . .

She smiles at me. AGAIN!

My mouth goes all weird.

I have no idea what to say.

"Hello," she says, "I'm Crystal. Thank you for stopping me from spinning."

"Gimble flug hurk murgle bindo flam fluge," I say.

She looks at me as if I'm made of

spare jellyfish parts. "Do you speak Finglish?" Crystal asks with a grin so perfect you could frame it and put it on the wall.

"He used to," says Ralph, "up until about thirty seconds ago."

Deep inside my head, I find my name. I'm about to say it when Harvey, realizing he's no longer the center of attention, bounces on one side of my hammer. But that's not the worst part. That's when Harvey starts shouting, at the top of his gills, "HARRY'S GOT A GIRLFRIEND! YUCK, YUCK, YUCKITTY YUCK! HARRY'S GOT A GIRLFRIEND! YUCK!"

Crystal looks as embarrassed as I do, and heads off with a swish of her tail to rejoin her pod.

All I'm left with is Harvey, laughing so much he sounds like he might make himself sick. And I remind myself that this is still just the first day of vacation with Harvey.

Now I'm more determined than ever to find the secret resting place of the Black Blood Pearl . . . so that I can hide my horrible little cousin there!

CHAPTER 3

"Welcome to Treasure Reef!" Captain Pike calls through the ferry's loudspeaker as we pull into the harbor.

The waves of the Diamond Sea glitter for sixty fathoms over our heads, sending dazzling slivers of light through the currents. The water is warm and tropical, and smells of food from the restaurants carved into the coral reef ahead of us.

As we get off the ferry, Ralph closes his eyes and floats blindly toward the aromas.

"I'm in heaven," he whispers.

"I wanna sandy-floss!" screams Harvey, pointing to an angelfish in a white hat making pink, fluffy, sandy-floss.

"We'll get you some when we get to the hotel," Aunt Hettie promises.

Harvey folds his fins and thumps his tail up and down until Uncle Hector takes out his wallet and buys him a huge sandy-floss.

Dad organizes a taxicrab to take us to our hotel.

As we wind through the coral streets we pass several shops selling Long Fin Silver merchandise and it cheers me up immediately. I can't wait to break out some of my saved-up allowance and buy myself some cool pirate gear.

Operation Black Blood Pearl—which I just named—is nearly ready to go!

"What a dump!"

We pull up outside the Hotel Barracuda,

and Harvey can't control himself. We climb out of the wheezing old taxicrab and I can't really disagree with him.

The Hotel Barracuda is carved deep into the last mountain of Treasure Reef, just before the shelf falls away sharply into the dangerous depths of the Diamond Sea. It looks as spooky and creepy as a hotel from a horror movie. Even being named after Long Fin Silver's infamous pirate ship is not enough to make it look inviting.

An old, wrinkly sea turtle wearing a manager's badge meets us at the entrance. "Welcome," he says in

a whispery voice. "I'm Hank, the hotel manager. I hope you'll enjoy your stay with us . . . however long it might last." Hank piles our bags onto his back and limps up the stairs.

The Hotel Barracuda looks like the inside of a shipwreck. Gloomy and cold and covered in weeds and barnacles. The stairs leading to the upper levels are as old and as creaky as Hank. Dad starts congratulating Hank on the "atmosphere and sense of history" inside the hotel. Hank doesn't answer. He just keeps on staring straight ahead like he's thinking about something really serious. He's the creepiest, saddest turtle I've ever met.

When we finally get to our floor, Aunt Hettie and Uncle Hector rush into their room and slam the door hard.

I look at Mom.

I look at Dad.

I look at Harvey. Why haven't they taken him?

Harvey whoops and darts into my room. Through the open door I see him swim upward, yelling, "I call top bunk!"

Mom whispers, "Sorry, but it's your aunt and uncle's anniversary, remember?"

Dad pretends to be looking something up on his octopiPAD.

Hank takes Mom and Dad's things into their room, leaving Ralph and me in the corridor with only one way to go—into the room with Harvey.

Ralph looks at me.

I look at Ralph.

"Make the jellyvision work, Harry!" Harvey yells. "I wanna watch *Shark Point's Got Talent!*"

Luckily, by the time we've unpacked, it's dinnertime.

Ralph, Harvey, and I follow the grown-ups down to the dining room. It's just as dumpy as the rest of the hotel.

We all look at the menu. Harvey demands a sandy-floss starter, with a sandy-floss main, and double krill-cream and sandy-floss for dessert.

As I read my way down the menu, I feel a fin in my ribs. Ralph's trying to get my attention.

"Look!"

I glance up from the menu. Coming through the doors are Crystal and the rest of the dolphin girls, followed by their parents.

I just stare.

I must look crazy.

I HAVE TO GET A GRIP!

I have a treasure to find! I can't lose my focus. *Concentrate, Hammerskull. Keep your eyes on the prize.*

But as soon as Harvey notices Crystal looking at me, he stops complaining to Aunt Hettie about being made to order sea-vegetables, and twists his hammer into the shape of a love heart.

"Oooooh, Crystal!" he teases. "Here's your boyfriend, Harry. Come say hello!"

Crystal hides behind her friends, and Mom gives me a harsh look for hissing at Harvey. But before I can complain, the

47

dining room's plunged into almost total darkness.

I jump, and a shivering Ralph tries to swim under my left fin.

"W-w-w-what's going on?" he stammers.

If the hotel had looked spooky in the daylight, it's nothing compared to how it looks now.

A single spotlight hits a pair of long seaweed curtains, which open up to reveal a wide stage. Hank the Turtle is standing there behind a rusty microphone.

"Ladies and gentlemen," Hank mumbles into the mic. "It's time for the cabaret." He sounds nervous and tense. Maybe he

knows how awful the acts are and he's worried about the complaints he's going to get!

Hank limps off the stage, and the show begins.

The show is just as rundown and ratty as the hotel.

First up are Lobsters Eleven—a dance troupe in faded sequins who perform to the worst music ever. I know it's terrible because Dad taps his tail along to it as he eats, and claps like an octopus when they finish. My dad has legendarily bad taste in music, so you know that if he likes something, it's going to stink.

Next on stage is someone Hank introduces as the Great Tentaclops, who is majorly ungreat. He's an ancient gray-green octopus wearing a red wig that keeps slipping around his big, shiny head.

He starts singing a song called "My Sea-Way," by someone called Frank Finatra.

Mom and Dad love it.

I just sit here yawning. Ralph darts in and out of my mouth to grab bits of food, and Harvey keeps swimming under the table to tickle my dorsal!

When will this night ever end?

When will I be able to start searching for the Black Blood Pearl?

And will Crystal ever smile at me again?

I thought Treasure Reef was supposed to be the best vacation spot in the ocean. And this was supposed to be the most awesome vacation ever.

So far, it was the worst.

CHAPTER 4

"Listen carefully," Ralph says to me the following morning. "I'm about to give you a list of all the things I want you to have for breakfast. Number one: Kelp Krispies. Number two: cod-eggs-over-easy. Three: streaky whale bacon. Four: an extra-large helping of halibut hash browns. Five: all washed down with a glass of—"

"Ralph, stop! Number one: It's *my* breakfast. And number two: I do the lists."

Ralph stops on the spooky staircase and frowns at me. "Harry, this is my vacation too, and it's my breakfast too. I want you to eat that stuff so I can pick out the leftovers from between your teeth. Okay?"

Before I can reply, Harvey tears past us, screaming, "BREAKFAST!" He's going so fast Ralph and I are sent hurtling back up the stairs in his wake. If only we were on the actual *Barracuda*, instead of this rickety hotel named after it. At least then we could trick Harvey into climbing up to the sea-crow's nest so we wouldn't have to lay eyes on him.

But then as Ralph and I mope our way downstairs, the weirdest thing happens. A wailing sound starts coming from the dining room. At first I think it must be Harvey making more trouble, but then I see that the dining room is full of guests gathered around Hank. Some are holding up empty octi-purses and suitcases.

"Everything is gone! All my jewelfish-jewelry!" An elderly squid cries, her tentacles trembling.

"My diamond necklace-fish is missing too!" a young reef shark says.

Hank holds up his forefeet, trying to calm the crowd. "Please, everyone, settle down."

A dressed-up monkfish holds up an empty jewelry box. "I saw someone! A thief leaving my room with my pearls!"

"What? Well then, why didn't you stop him?" a clown fish demands.

"Because," the monkfish begins quietly. "Because, it was the *ghost of Long Fin Silver!*" the monkfish replies, trembling with fear.

Everyone gasps.

Especially me.

Hank's face falls an entire fathom.

A terrified-looking bull shark chimes in, "Yes! I saw the ghost too. It was clanking and moaning down the corridor, waving its wooden fin and gleaming sword!"

The ghost of Long Fin Silver? Here in the hotel?

Hang on.

I don't believe in ghosts.

This has to be fake.

"My mom saw the ghost too!" says a voice that I recognize immediately. Crystal swims to the front of the shoal. "Just after he took her rings and barnacle bracelets."

"Everyone calm down! You must stay calm!"

Oh no, this is just what we *don't* need.

Dad appears from behind the crowd, floating onto a table and addressing the guests like he's addressing a meeting of the Shark Point Council.

Please, floor. Open up now. Swallow me whole.

"It's the mayor of Shark Point!" someone says. Unbelievably, the crowd turns from Hank to Dad and actually starts to listen.

"Fellow guests, I have already spoken to Hank, the owner of this charming hotel, long before you discovered the thefts of your precious jewelry. You see, my wife and I were also visited by the ghost of Long Fin Silver last night, but luckily we disturbed him before he could make off with any of our prized possessions."

Dad, you're only making it worse.
A cheer goes up from the group.
WHAT?????
"That's lucky!" one of them calls.

"Well done!" says another.

I look at Ralph.

Ralph shrugs.

Harvey looks around for Kelp Krispies.

"Hank tells me that he is very sorry for what has happened," Dad continues.

Hank nods and I think I see tears in the corners of his eyes. "It's been happening all summer," he says sadly. "But this is the worst night yet. If news gets out, we're going to go out of business and lose everything! And who knows what will happen to all of Treasure Reef!"

"We can't let that happen, can we?" Dad shakes his fin in determination. "As public-spirited citizens we're not going to stand for this, are we?"

Yes, Dad. Yes they are.

"No!" shouts everyone. "No we're not!"

I look at Ralph.

Ralph double-shrugs.

Harvey has found some of last night's sandy-floss on a table at the back of the dining room and is eating it happily.

"I say we help Hank keep his hotel by keeping our eyes open and our sonars peeled," Dad says. "And if we do that, I'm sure we'll not only be able to stop this from happening again, but we'll also be able to recover all your lost jewelry."

62

The cheers from the guests are so loud they make the coral-carved windows rattle in their frames.

Unbelievable.

"Shhhhhh! Keep your voice down!" I flap my fin over Ralph's mouth and look up at the top bunk, where I hope Harvey's still napping off his enormous sandy-floss breakfast. I remove my fin from Ralph's face.

"But how is staking out the reception area of the ocean's creepiest hotel at midnight going to help you find the Black

Blood Pearl?" he whispers. "It doesn't make any sense!"

Well it all makes perfect sense to me. I give Ralph a quick list.

1. We'll be in the best place to see the ghost of Long Fin Silver.
2. He has to go through the lobby to get to the rooms.
3. We can follow him.

(Ralph looks quite pale at the idea of following a ghost. I carry on with my list. . . .)

4. Once he's robbed some jewelry, one of two things will happen.

"I can think of a *million* things that will happen," Ralph interrupts, "all bad, and about three quarters of them involve being SCARED TO DEATH!"

"As I said, one of two things will happen—One: The ghost is *real*—so we follow him back to his lair and find out where the Black Blood Pearl is buried.

"Well, that sounds safe," Ralph says. "NOT!"

"Two: He's not a real ghost, but he is

a real jewel thief—so we follow him back to his hideout and get all the jewels back and become *heroes!*

"I WANNA FOLLOW THE GHOST!"

The sides of my hammer droop with disappointment. Harvey is sitting up in his bunk, his eyes glimmering with excitement.

"I wanna come," he whines.

"You can't," I say. I think *Number 3: Harvey will spoil everything. He won't be able to keep quiet. He'll be looking for someone to annoy or food to eat.*

"Okay, then," Harvey says, getting out of bed, pulling on his robe, and heading for the door.

"Really?" I say, stunned.

"Really," says Harvey with a grin, opening the door.

"It's a trap," says Ralph.

"Where are you going, Harvey?" I ask, stopping the door with the end of my hammer.

"Just going to tell Mom, Dad, and Uncle Hugo exactly what you're planning tonight, and that you've both been

calling me names and making me cry and won't let me go to sleep!"

"Told you," says Ralph. "A trap."

It's almost midnight and the hotel lobby is totally silent.

Apart from the creaking of the floorboards as they settle in the night . . .

Apart from the chill ocean currents whistling past the windows like the dread calls of the lost . . .

Apart from the grandfather clock in the corner, ticking away like it's counting down to the appearance of an unspeak-able terror . . .

Apart from Harvey, who's chomping on a seaberry-ripple and asking, "So when's this ghost pirate gonna turn up, Haz?"

He's started calling me Haz because apparently it "takes too long" to say Harry. Or even Harry Hammerskull.

Ralph is hiding behind me because he's too scared to look.

But Harvey? He is swimming from side to side flashing his angler-fish torch, not even looking the slightest bit nervous.

Ahead of us and behind us, hall-
ways stretch off into the darkness, their
waters getting chillier by the second.

Maybe Ralph is right.

Maybe this is a bad idea.

"Got another seaberry-ripple, Haz
Hammerskull?"

"No."

"What have you got?"

*A ferry ride home, if you're not care-
ful,* I think to myself. "Nothing!" I hiss.

"You're a goon! A goofy goon! RGNG-
NGNGHHHHH!"

I grab Harvey and put my hammer over his mouth. "Please be quiet!

Silver's ghost isn't going to appear if you're going to keep begging for ice cream!"

Poink!!!!

Ralph pokes me in the dorsal. "Harry!"

"Wait, I'm dealing with Harvey! He's nibbling my hammer and it hurts!"

Poink!!!!

"Ralph! Stop it!"

Poink!!!!

Poink!!!!

Poink!!!!

"Ow!" I yell, letting go of Harvey and spinning around to look at Ralph. But . . .

"ARRRRRRRRRRRRRRRGHHH!"

yells Harvey, seeing what I see, now
that his face is out of my hammer.

"NOOOOOOOOOOOOOOOOOOOO!"
yells Ralph, putting his fins over his
eyes.

"Oh my cod," I whisper.

At the end of the corridor—huge, glowing green, and rattling a pirate's sword—comes the terrifying sight of Long Fin Silver's ghost. It's floating straight toward us, moaning.

"YO ... HO ... HO ... !"

WHOOOOOOOOOOOOOOOOOOSH!!!

Silver's ghost flashes past us in a rush of cold water and a green glow.

It moans its way through the lobby toward the dining room. I drag Ralph and Harvey along behind me as I follow. "Silver! Silver!" I call to the mysterious apparition. "Where's the Black Blood Pearl? Please tell me!"

Silver's shoulders hunch and he seems to speed up. . . .

There's a strange smell in the water that I don't recognize, but it definitely wasn't there before the ghost wafted past.

I see Silver's green glow in the dining room, then suddenly it blinks off as if a phantom switch has been flicked.

When I finally drag Ralph and the protesting Harvey through the dining room door, Silver's ghost has completely disappeared!

CHAPTER 5

"It *had* to be a ghost," I say to Ralph the next morning on the way down to breakfast. "We looked everywhere for it—and it was totally gone."

"I don't care if it's a ghost or not. I don't want to see it ever again!" says Ralph as we enter the dining room.

"I WANNA DOUBLE CHOC-BAIT SUNDAE FOR BREAKFAST!" yells Harvey. How much food can one little shark eat?

Just like yesterday, the dining room is full of unhappy hotel guests. Only this time Dad isn't trying to calm anyone down.

"Silver's ghost stole my octopiPAD!" he wails.

It turns out Silver's ghost stole even *more* possessions last night. Hank is beside himself with worry, promising free vacations to everyone who's had stuff stolen.

I think about telling Dad I saw the ghost last night but decide not to. It's not as if we caught him or recovered the stolen goods. I'll get into trouble for being out of my room late at night. And I'll get into even worse trouble for taking Harvey with me.

And I don't plan on telling him we're after the Black Blood Pearl.

"Shall we go into town and buy some snacks?" I say to Ralph. "I don't think breakfast's going to be served anytime soon."

Ralph nods eagerly.

"I wanna come too!" Harvey whines.

He swims up to my ear and whispers into it. "If you don't take me, I'll tell my mom and dad you made me go ghost-hunting last night and I almost *died*."

I'm about to make a list of all the reasons why I hate Harvey, but then my stomach starts to rumble. "Okay," I hiss. "Let's go."

We tell our parents what we're doing and swim toward the hotel entrance. A huge shadow falls across us. The Not-So-Great-Tentaclops is floating in the doorway. He's scratching his head with one tentacle, while holding what looks like a map with two others.

"Excuse me," I say as we try to squeeze past him. He reeks of the strongest aftershave I've ever smelled—it's making my eyes water. "Can we get past please, Mr. Tentaclops?"

Tentaclops looks up from the map. "Yeah, sure, kid."

As he moves aside, the morning light glitters on the surface of the map.

I see that it's a very old chart of Treasure Reef.

I can't help noticing that marked in one corner of it is a big *X* next to the letters "B. B. P."

Doink!

Ralph has seen it too. He mouths "*B. B. P.*," at me and then equally silently, his lips make the shapes for: BLACK BLOOD PEARL!!!!!!

I nod excitedly and look up at Tentaclops.

"Er, excuse me, Mister . . . what is that map?"

Tentaclops shrugs three of his shoulders. "Dunno, kid. Found it outside my room this morning. I hate people who drop litter, don't you?"

I nod, but at the same time I'm thinking, *Was it dropped by Long Fin Silver's ghost?*

"If it's garbage, shall I put it in the trash for you?" I ask nervously.

Tentaclops nods and hands me the map. "I can't make head nor beak of it, sonny—knock yourself out."

Tentaclops heads off and I look down

at the map like it's the most precious thing in the world . . . BECAUSE IT IS! Hammerskull is about to discover the greatest treasure of the seven seas!

"ARRGGGHHH!!!!! Haz! Help me! HELP ME!!" Harvey screams as the riptide drags him up and over the reef!

Wait.

What?

How did we get here?!

Okay. I don't have a lot of time to explain, so here's a quick list. . . .

1. Me, Harvey, and Ralph have some breakfast in the Treasure Reef Diner.

2. We study the map so closely it makes my eyes hurt. (Harvey isn't interested in the map. He has the ocean's largest choc-bait sundae, while Ralph and I plan our route up into the Coral Mountains to the B. B. P.)

3. After breakfast we head up the Coral Hills behind the hotel, getting more excited by the second. I can smell the treasure!

4. The map takes us up and up toward the shallows of the Diamond Sea. Ralph is a little bit scared. I put on my brave Hammerskull pirate face (including fin-patch) and lead the way with my swordlike tail.

5. When we reach the top of the mountain, the sea's surface is only two tail-lengths above our heads! But we're soooooooooooooo close to the big **X** on the map!
6. We get to the **X**.
7. We start to dig. . . .
8. "ARRGGGHHH!!!!! Haz! Help me! HELP ME!!" screams Harvey.

Okay, we're caught up now.

The map hasn't led us to the treasure of all treasures. . . .

It's led us into some really dangerous riptides!

Harvey, who isn't used to water

moving this fast, is being dragged away!

I drop the shovel and power my tail as hard as I can.

"Ralph!" I call. "Go back to the hotel and tell Mom and Dad!"

In the middle of all the commotion a swirl and whirl of a riptide knocks me over, and the treasure map goes swooshing away.

Gone and lost forever.

Now, you would think that Harry Hammerskull would be shouting and yelling that his glorious treasure was never to be found.

But that was the old Harry Hammer-skull.

The new Harry Hammerskull?

I don't care about long-lost stolen pearls.

I don't care about goofy treasure.

I don't care about dorky pirates.

All I care about?

Saving High-Seas-Harvey!

Out of the corner of my hammer I see Ralph swimming back down the coral slope into safer waters, hopefully on the way to my parents.

I'm swept out toward the rapidly disappearing Harvey.

There's no way I can swim
fast enough through the churn-
ing water to catch up with him. I *have* to
think of something.

Ding!

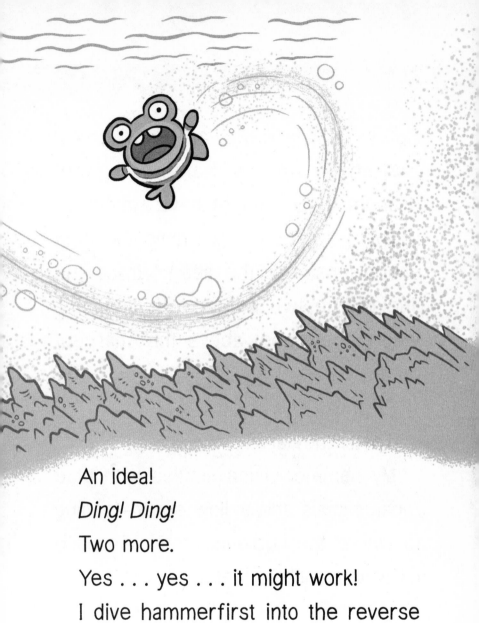

An idea!

Ding! Ding!

Two more.

Yes . . . yes . . . it might work!

I dive hammerfirst into the reverse

riptide, pulling me *away* from Harvey! Switching on my hammer-vision, (Hammerheads might have ridiculous rubbery heads, but we have the best shark-senses in the sea.) I trace the line of the two currents, looking for where they meet above the sharpest coral.

Ping!

There they are!

My hammer-vision sizzles with blue radar signals and yellow sonar—leading to where the currents crash into each other in a rushing whirlpool.

WHAM!!!!

I crash into the whirlpool.

SWOOOOOOOOOOOOOOSH!!!!

I let it take me, hard, around and around. . . .

Ping! goes my hammer-vision as I focus on Harvey's tiny shadow.

I begin the most vital countdown of my life.

FIVE!

FOUR!!

THREE!!!

TWO!!!!

ONE!!!!!

ZERO!!!!!!

I dig my left hammer into the wall of whirling water—which crashes my hammer-vision software immediately.

My body jackknifes straight-out into the bright, waterless air—just a dark speck of boy-shark sailing across the endless blue of the sky.

I try to remember *EXACTLY* where I last spotted Harvey with my hammer-vision. I twist a three-sixty nose-fluke straight into the sickest dorsal-wing and fin-propeller! I turn in the air, flip over, come crashing back into the waves, and . . .

BANGWASSSSSSSSSSSSSSSSSHHH-HHHAPPPPP!!!!

Harvey is in my fins, and the force of my splashdown pushes us both away from the rushing riptides over our heads and . . .

WHOOOOOOPOOOOO-SWISH-WHOOOOPPPPPP!!!!

HARVEY IS SAFE!

"Thank you, Harry! Thank you!" Harvey hugs me tight. Just like he did when he was a baby shark. As we reach the safer, deeper waters, he looks up at me with the googliest, happiest hammer-eyes ever!

CHAPTER 6

"And now I will perform my greatest trick!
The Disappearing Cabinet of Doom!"

A gasp goes up from the hotel din-
ers as a spotlight hits a shabby cabinet
being wheeled onto the stage by the
Not-So-Great-Tentaclops.

The cabinet has pictures on the side

that look like they've been painted by a three-year-old lobster. They're supposed to show Long Fin Silver, but they look more like an accident in a squid-ink factory.

WIN!

"Into the Cabinet of Doom I will place various items," the Not-So-Great-Tentaclops says, as he opens the cabinet door and stuffs a potted coral inside. "Abra-barracuda!" He waves his magic frond around, then opens the door.

The potted coral is gone.

Everyone claps wildly, especially Dad.

In fact, Dad makes so much noise, whistling and whooping, that Tentaclops shades his eyes against the spotlight and waves over at him. Then his huge glassy eyes spot me and he takes a sharp breath. I guess he's feeling guilty about giving us the map that sent us off into such danger, and didn't even lead us to the Black Blood Pearl.

Tentaclops continues shoving things into his cabinet and making them disappear.

I tried to catch Crystal's eye. She's sitting at the next table with her family, but she's too busy looking at Tentaclops.

Poink. Ralph fins me in the side.

I ignore him and start folding a napkin into a stingray shape, ready to launch it toward Crystal to get her attention.

Poink!

"Ralph!"

"I've had an idea," he says.

I sigh and put the napkin down.

"What is it?"

Ralph swims closer to me. "You know last night when Long Fin Silver's ghost came into the dining room and then completely disappeared?"

I nod.

"Well, what if he went into that Cabinet of Doom thingy?"

"Huh?"

"It's just a stupid trick, right?"

"Yes."

"So, those things that Tentaclops is

putting in there must be going some-where . . . maybe, just maybe, it's where the ghost went too!"

It doesn't take me two seconds to realize that Ralph has a point.

"We need to get a look inside that cabinet, Ralph."

But before we can do anything, Tentaclops runs out of things to make disappear, so he stuffs himself in the cabinet and slams the door. There's a muffled "Abrabarracuda!" from inside the cabinet. Then the door swings back open and, shazam! The cabinet is empty.

The crowd goes wild, the stage curtains close, and Hank floats up onto a chair. "Sharks and crustaceans, I would like to thank you all for your kind support during this difficult time. . . ."

As Hank drones on, Ralph and I dart under the tables and head for the stage.

Ralph pulls aside the curtain, and we dive behind it. Backstage is dimly lit, and we can only just hear the voices and clapping beyond the curtains. What I can smell, immediately, is Tentaclops's horrible aftershave. It lingers in the water like bad bottom-toots.

Covering my nose with a fin, I approach the Cabinet of Doom.

Close-up, the pictures of Long Fin Silver are even more pathetic and childish.

I slowly open the cabinet and peek inside. The stench of Tentaclops is even worse.

Holding my nose, I swim in.

The walls, the floor, and the top of the cabinet all seem pretty solid. I can't see how anything, let alone Tentaclops, managed to disappear from inside here.

"Where's Harry, Ralph?"

Oh no! It's Mom! She must have stuck

her head through the curtain. Ralph slams the cabinet door shut and suddenly I'm in total darkness.

"I don't know, Mrs. Hammerhead," I hear Ralph say. "Maybe he's gone back to his room. He must be really tired after today."

"Ah, that's a shame, his dad's about to make a speech."

I hear the curtain swoosh back into place, so I reach out to push the door open, but in the darkness I can't find the handle. As I fumble about with my fin, there's a click, and . . .

Bam!!!!

103

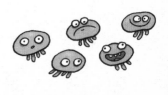

The floor beneath me falls away. But I balance on the ledge and see a long, rocky tunnel lit by an eerie green glow. It leads right down under the hotel.

I get a whiff of Tentaclops's after-shave, but strangely I can smell the same weird smell I noticed when Long Fin Silver's ghost appeared!

Ralph was right. This must have been how the ghost escaped.

I should go down there, shouldn't I?

I should go to check if Tentaclops is okay.

But it's really scary, and cold and green and glowy.

Harry Hammer would never be brave enough to go down there.

But . . . the Dread Pirate Harry Hammerskullandcrossbones would go down there like a shot!

I push my tail-like sword forward and whisper, "Yo, ho, ho." I crank my Pirate Courage to maximum and drop down into the tunnel!

Down, down, deeper and deeper I go. The green glow gets greener and the weird smell gets stronger. Eventually the tunnel opens up into a wide cavern. The water is cold and stagnant and deathly quiet.

Even Harry Hammerskull is getting a bit creeped out, but I've come too far to turn back now. I have to go on.

As I reach the back of the cavern, something glimmers and catches my

eye. The glimmer is red and it's blinking beneath a pile of coral and seaweed.

I reboot my hammer-vision and use it to scan beneath the coral.

Leaping into focus, sharp-edged and flat-screened, is my dad's octopiPAD!

I quickly move the coral and seaweed out of the way.

And there, in the sand, is not only my dad's octopiPAD, but the jewels stolen by Long Fin Silver's ghost! I move the octopi-PAD to one side and start collecting finfuls of jewelry. Suddenly my hammer-vision almost *pings* my hammer off! It's picking up something round buried deep below the surface.

I start to dig.

And dig.

And dig.

And just when I almost stop digging, something rolls out from beneath a rock. It's black and beautiful and the most amazing treasure I've seen on this entire vacation.

Could it be?

No!

Could it?

It must be! It's the BLACK BLOOD PEARL!

I'VE FOUND IT!!!

108

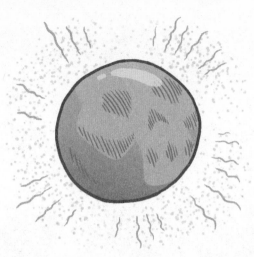

I hold the pearl up to my hammer, looking deep into its shiny black surface. I can almost hear the voices of the baroness of sharks and the king of sands as they curse Long Fin Silver for stealing the pearl and ruining their love forever!

"GIVE ME BACK THAT PEARL! IT'S MINE!"

I spin around to see Long Fin Silver's ghost glowing green through the gloom.

My heart does seventeen nosedives in my chest. Silver's sword slices through the water toward me.

I have to get out of here right now!

Kicking up a cloud of sand to hide my escape route, I clutch the Black Blood Pearl and Dad's octopiPAD in my fins and swim as fast as I can toward the tunnel.

"Come back, you little thief!" Silver's ghost booms as he whooshes after me.

With no time to waste, I carve a sharp semicircle through the water and dive hammerfirst up the tunnel, trying not to scrape my back against the sharp coral walls.

I can feel Silver's breath on my tail as I kick.

"Give me that pearl! It's mine, I tell

you! Mine! I've been searching for it for years!"

I swim on, kicking harder than I ever have before, going up and up toward the Cabinet of Doom.

Up . . .

and . . .

up . . .

and . . .

up . . .

until . . .

CRASHHHHHHHHHHHHHHHHHHH!!!!

I smack into the roof of the cabinet and almost knock myself out.

As I look down I see that Silver isn't

112

quick enough to brake, and I just manage to get out the of the way as he slams into the cabinet and . . . *KERRR-RRRRRRRRRRRRASHHHHHHH!!!!* . . . it disintegrates!

Silver and I cartwheel out of the shattered box, through the stage curtains, and burst into the dining room into the middle of the hotel guests.

Everyone starts to panic.

"Run! It's the ghost!" they cry. "THE GHOST!"

Holding the Black Blood Pearl and his octopiPAD, I rush toward Dad, who's still midspeech.

Long Fin Silver is in hot pursuit, his weird smell filling the water around me.

I crash sideways into a group of startled hotel staff-squids, getting totally tangled in their tentacles . . . and that's when the pearl and the octopiPAD fly out of my fins!

Dad ignores the pearl and dives straight for his octopiPAD.

The pearl bounces off his hammer . . . and lands right in the middle of Crystal's dinner!

Dad's tail slips sideways.

Silver crashes straight into it, and he gets tangled in the mass of squid legs beside me.

My heart is beating like it's going to bust out of my chest!

Luckily, the squids realize they've

116

caught the ghost, and they tighten their tentacles. Long Fin Silver tries to break free, but the more he wriggles, the more tangled he becomes. Then his sword floats away on the currents caused by the panicking guests. The same powerful currents start pulling the ghost's hair up, up, and . . .

Oh my cod! Long Fin Silver's hair floats away!

But he's a ghost! How can that even be possible???

What's left is a red-colored wig and the green head of . . . THE GREAT TENTACLOPS!

"Look, everyone!" I yell. "Tentaclops was the ghost all along!"

Half in and half out of his Long Fin Silver costume, Tentaclops is a pathetic sight. And now I know where the horrible smell is coming from. The ghost costume is covered in sticky, green, luminous paint. That must be why

Tentaclops wore so much aftershave—to try to cover the stink.

Everything is starting to make sense.

And *ding*!

I remember Tentaclops giving me the map.

He probably thought we knew he was behind all the thefts. He also probably believed we knew he was masquerading as the dreaded pirate Silver. But—we knew nothing until we discovered everything!

So Tentaclops faked the map to take us up to the dangerous riptides and get us out of the picture!

119

What a nasty piece of work.

"Hank," Dad calls, hugging his octopi-Pad. "I think we have your thief. I suggest you call the police and have him arrested. Do you have anything to say for yourself, Tentaclops?"

Tentaclops struggles in the tight tentacles. "I would have escaped if it hadn't been for those pesky squids! You were all foolish enough to believe I was the ghost of Long Fin Silver! I could have gotten away with the Black Blood Pearl— the greatest jewel of the sea!"

"Well done, Harry!" proclaims Dad. "You

exposed his evil stealing ways! You're a true hero!"

"Harry the Hero. Harry the Hero!" everyone in the dining room starts to chant. Ralph and Harvey each take one of my fins and hold them up in the water. Harvey starts dancing around as they all cry: **"HARRY THE HERO!!!!"**

After the police have taken Tentaclops away, Hank comes over and shakes me warmly by the fin. "Harry, I can't thank you enough for what you've done today,"

he says with a beaming grin. "Now that Tentaclops is behind bars, I've got the chance to make the Hotel Barracuda the success I've always wanted it to be. It'll be tough, but I'm going to give it my best shot."

"Oh, I don't think it'll be that tough, Hank," I say with a knowing smile.

"Really?"

"Yes." I turn and call out to Crystal.

"Yes, Harry," she says as she swims over.

"Show Hank what plopped onto your plate in all the commotion."

Crystal smiles broadly and holds out her fin.

The Black Blood Pearl gleams in the water.

"Is that—is that what I think it is?" Hank stammers.

"It sure is. The Black Blood Pearl was buried beneath your hotel, Hank. So it must belong to you. I bet every fish in the sea would come to see the famous Black Blood Pearl of Long Fin Silver on display!"

Hank's eyes fill with happy tears. "Harry, you've saved the Hotel Barracuda. How can I ever thank you?"

I think for just one second and then say, "How about fully loaded choc-bait sundaes for my mom, my dad, my aunt, my uncle, Crystal . . ."

Crystal smiles at me.

I smile at Crystal.

"And . . ."

"I WANNA CHOC-BAIT SUNDAE!" cries Harvey.

"High-Seas-Harvey," I say, and give an even bigger smile to the most annoying, pesky, and unforgettable little cousin in the deep blue sea.

THE END

Meet Harry and the Shark Point gang. . . .

HARRY

Species:

hammerhead shark

You'll spot him . . .

using his special

hammer-vision

Favorite thing:

his Gregor the Gnasher

poster

Most likely to say:

"I wish I was a great white."

Most embarrassing moment: when Mom called him

her "little starfish" in front of all his friends

RALPH

Species:

pilot fish

You'll spot him . . .

eating the food from

between Harry's teeth!

Favorite thing: shrimp Pop-Tarts

Most likely to say: "So, Harry, what's for

breakfast today?"

Most embarrassing moment: eating too much cake

on Joe's birthday. His face was COVERED in pink

plankton icing.

JOE

Species: jellyfish

You'll spot him . . . hiding behind Ralph and Harry, or behind his own tentacles

Favorite thing: his cave, since it's nice and safe

Most likely to say: "If we do this, we're going to end up as fish food. . . ."

Most embarrassing moment: whenever his rear goes *toot*, which is when he's scared. Which is all the time.

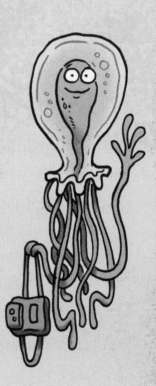

RICK

Species: blacktip reef shark

You'll spot him . . .

bullying smaller fish

or showing off

Favorite thing: his black

leather jacket

Most likely to say:

"Last one there's a sea snail!"

Most embarrassing moment:

none. Rick's far too cool to get embarrassed.